Scout Allen
Hot Lesbian Romance

Both Ways

Days of Temptation, Book 2

Days of Temptation, Book 2

Both Ways

Hot Lesbian Romance

By: Scout Allen

© **Scout Allen 2014**
ISBN: 978-1-62761-782-6

About the Publisher

4Fun Publishing, a member of **BLVNP Incorporated**, 340 S. Lemon #6200,
Walnut CA 91789, info@blvnp.com / legal@blvnp.com
NOTE: Due to the highly emotional reaction of some people to works of erotic
fiction, any email sent to the above address that contains foul language or
religious references is automatically deleted by our anti-spam software and will
not be seen. All other communications are welcome.

DISCLAIMER

Please don't be stupid and kill yourself. This book is a work of FICTION.
Do not try any new sexual practice that you find in this book. It is fiction and not
to be confused with reality. Neither the author nor the publisher or its associates
assume any responsibility for any loss, injury, death or legal consequences
resulting from acting on the contents in this book. Every character in this book is
over 18 years of age. The author's opinions are not to be construed as the
opinions of the publisher. The material in this book is for entertainment purposes
ONLY. Enjoy.

TIFFANY HAD told Lacy that we would join her in the Orgy she had planned for the end of the month.

We had agreed to it only if she guaranteed no one would fuck Tiffany's pussy; they say you can when you're pregnant but we really don't want to, especially with my size and well, imagining I might be jabbing the unborn child in the middle of a sexual orgasm. She said it wouldn't be a problem, she knew a lot of people who were going to it, mostly her friends and friends of theirs she had met. With the agreement set, we got dressed - as much as one does for an orgy - and we arrived at her home in the suburbs.

Being as the new, more permissive laws on public decency and the allowance of minimal clothing was still only five months old, people were still arriving in robes and long jackets to hide their bodies from the view of the world, myself included.

Except for Tiffany.

She took this new freedom wherever she could get it, reveling in the attention and the fact that nowadays, dressing to leave the house was something one could consider as optional rather than required. She wore a black, lacy baby-doll with a thong that she'd recently bought at the store, the strings on the back splitting up around her ass cheeks, with an X of red tape over her crotch. If anyone doubted that X, I would show them the errors of their ways.

We walked inside, allowing a man who was wearing a robe covered in pacman's, to go ahead of us. Inside people were in various states of dress and undress; I never knew lace could be put to so many uses. I suddenly felt very self-conscious in my white boy shorts underneath my white robe with hearts all around the waist. My penis however had no problem with this as she was getting erect under the fabric, and my bare and unsupported breasts were ready for some attention.

Tiffany took off my robe and hung it up without asking me, because we'd agreed upon this beforehand. My cheeks were blushing as we walked around the rooms. I saw some familiar faces, and a few that I knew I'd already seen partially or completely naked at work numerous times. The others were just as dressed and just as friendly. They came in all body types too; our office, it seemed, was the only one that had instituted the exercise before work program.

My erection strained against my boxers and my cheeks were bright red because of her. Many people saw, a few of them giving me looks after that but the rest just seemed to be sizing me up because of it, both men and women.

Tiffany was smiling at everyone and greeting those she knew, basically acting like she was the hostess of the party instead of Lacy. I didn't mind, she could be the socialite while I blushed behind her and tried to keep my eyes off of every exposed pussy, dick, ass, chests, arms, breasts…whoa calm down girl.

"You ok, honey?" Tiffany gave me a concerned look.

"Yeah," I said blushing even more, if that was possible, "I'm just nervous, not many people know what I am."

She gripped my erection and planted a kiss directly on my lips in front of everyone. Her lips tasted like cherry and her smell drifted up into my nose, making me shudder in response. I was more than a little horny after she broke the kiss. "You're beautiful." She gave me an extra squeeze for emphasis. "Show them just how beautiful you are," she added, and with that she turned around and walked forward proudly holding my hand.

She's amazing.

We found Lacy lying on her front on the kitchen table getting a massage. Her ebony skin and black hair showed off her wide ass and long toned legs, making me quiver with anticipation. She was with a man in a harness made of belts running over both his shoulders, underneath his pecs, which were firm and hard, to connect on his chest. Another belt going down from that junction to his waist where another belt came around his waist and a third belt came up from his cock which was poking through a ring stiff and erect while his balls hung behind it strapped up against him with the belt. He was a ruggedly handsome, ripped man servant, and she was treating him as such.

"Deeper into my shoulder blades, slave," she said with little care.

"Yes ma'am," he said and his cock gave an appreciative twitch from the order.

She looked up and smiled at Tiffany, "Oh! I'm so glad you came! Where's Steph?"

"Here," I said and came around so we were face to crotch.

She chose to look at my penis while she talked. "I'd love to see that monster, Steph."

Tiffany, ever helpful, reached in the boxer slot and pulled out my rock hard cock and pushed me forward. Her hands touched it immediately and she grinned, "So hard and stiff."

Looking around the people who were now watching with muted interest, I said, "It's kind of hard not to be around here - AHH!" She'd taken me in her mouth, shocking me.

It seemed to signal a start to the festivities as everyone openly or shyly began to masturbate, some cocks came out while others simply removed what little clothing they were wearing. I made eye contact with a woman who was watching Lacy tonguing my cock with lust-filled eyes.

"I'll leave you to it," said Tiffany as she kissed me on the cheek and left.

Worried about her and the men here, although my mind was having trouble keeping focus, I watched that ass of hers as she sauntered off, spurring me into thrusting into Lacy's mouth.

Looking up, I noticed her man servant hadn't stopped massaging her naked form, but a little bit of precum had begun to leak out of his penis at the sight of it and he smiled at me, but said nothing.

A woman of Asian descent came toward us. She was wearing a black lace teddy that was basically two ribbons of lace that ran down over her breasts, leaving a window from mid-boob to just above her belly button with only a string running around the back. She wore a matching thong that was split down the middle leaving two triangles to show off her pretty pussy. And as if it would hide who she was she also wore a black lace mask around her eyes, leaving the rest of her face bare.

It made for quite the erotic sight. She came over boldly, whether because of the lust in the air or because of her mask it didn't matter. This was what the night was for: fun, no-strings-attached, sex. She grabbed my breast with a fierce grip and squeezed tight, making me take in a breath. I pulled her forward and kissed her on the lips, and she grabbed my back and pressed my breasts into hers.

As I grabbed her ass and squeezed, she pressed her crotch up against my leg and began to rub her bare pussy against it, slowly. The combined groping of her hand on my breast and Lacy's tongue bath sent me over the edge into my first climax of the night, shooting deep down her throat and beyond.

My kiss intensified ten-fold as my hips trust into her with a force not my own. My nerves were lit up, my emotions of lust and animal passion flying freely as we finished out kiss and I pulled out of her mouth. Lacy wouldn't have it though and cleaned me up quickly.

The Asian woman spoke with an accent that just sent me wild. "You hard no more," she pouted like only women of her ethnicity can, "I wanted to feel you inside."

After Lacy finished cleaning me off I was rock hard again. Pulling away from her grip, I grabbed the Asian woman tightly around the waist. "I'm not a man, darling."

My sex-drive was in the driver's seat while animal lust and need was its co-driver, changing me into a confident, in control, naked hermaphrodite.

Lifting her up onto the counter, I opened her lips and then looked at her as she was smiling gleefully. Thrusting slowly at first then quicker I touched my finger to her button and masturbated her furiously as I filled her to the hilt again and again. She was moaning out loud as her nipples hardened against the fabric.

"Yes, yes... Harder, faster!"

Her accent was driving me wild, making me feel like I was deflowering some Asian virgin. Her tight, silky walls spurred me on. They were tight as a hand, sending a shudder of pleasure through my cock with each thrust.

Someone spread my ass cheeks and I turned to see a man there smiling. Although a little hairy and with a gut, he knew what he was doing as he licked my asshole. I stood still for a moment as the thought that a strange tongue was on my asshole ran through my mind.

"Don't stop!" the Asian woman cried out in front of me, her hand replacing my stopped one.

Spreading my legs wider, I thrust again and her eyes closed as she continued moaning, spurring me on with 'Fuck yes' and 'Oooohhh' through clenched teeth.

The man behind me had his tongue reached deep inside, and I groaned out loud. With a long, hard thrust into her, his tongue retreated, and looking back mournfully, I found he was still smiling at me as he replaced it with his fingers. Turning my attention back to the woman in front of me, I saw she was smiling contently, her face aglow. She was grinning as her pussy leaked juice all over my fingers. Wow, she'd come without me even knowing it... the man behind me was good.

Not feeling quite done with her velvet lock, though, I angled my cock at her entrance and continued on as her eyes went wide open and she started gasping once more, along with my own moans and groans. She popped a breast out of her outfit and began kneading it roughly. Latching my mouth onto her chest, I began to suck and twirl my tongue around her erect nipple, barely conscious of what I was doing. I was running purely on animal lust and sexual instinct.

I soon felt my back entrance invaded by not fingers but a cock! My body convulsed into its second orgasm, bringing my head back and making me scream out loud as I came deep in my Asian fucker. Coming down from that high I could still feel the cock, an actual cock, not a dildo, or a strapon, fucking my ass.

"Yes, oh yes!" riding him to his release, I sighed and slid down to the floor, my ass leaking cum and my dick, quickly shrinking, covered in the juices of both me and my Asian lover.

Smiling like a Cheshire cat, I simply sat there while my batteries recharged a bit. He left me like we'd simply had a conversation, and in a way we did, and went in search of a new conquest. She slid down and sat beside me, grinning madly. "Best fuck had," she said in that cute sexy voice.

Touching her thigh, I nodded. It was not my best but, "Pretty damn good." All we could do was watch the surrounding couples, and not-couples, going at it in the kitchen.

A man and woman, both quite fit and sexy were simply fucking on the floor doggy style, her face not a foot from my crotch, but she was in no state to do anything about it, not to mention her other hand was busy between her own legs.

Two naked guys were kissing each other deeply against the counter. They looked like they were a couple, unless the two half-dressed women who had made their way onto the counter behind the guys and started making out, were somehow their girlfriends. One of the women had a torn bra on her left breast while the other was half wearing a slutty black dress that would have been hugging her curves if not for the slit up the side, or was it a tear? The one on bottom reached out and grasped one guy's erection and began jacking him. He noticed, and so did the other guy, but only for a moment; they just went back to making out, rubbing their genitals together.

Looking to my far left, there was a sight that made me horny all over again, although my little girl was still recovering from her fucking earlier. I meant my dick, not the Asian woman. One girl was in the middle of a gangbang, one cock in her mouth, another in her crotch from a guy below her and a black guy fucking her from behind with what looked like a cock equal to mine. The guy whose cock she was sucking looked old enough to be her father, but she didn't care, or couldn't voice her objection as he was balls deep in her all too willing mouth.

Finding my legs and getting up, I saw Lacy was now on her back and her slave-man, whose cock was still erect, was at her face and she was giving him a tongue bath, very excruciatingly slow, as his face was somewhere between pleasure and pain, and he was reaching back and inserting a dildo into her pussy rapidly. It was a rabbit that was touching her clit with each thrust, and it was vibrating. She seemed to be having fun, in both senses, but that made me feel a little bad for the slave, although he made no attempt to stop his mistress, or beg her to let him cum. In fact he seemed harder than a steel rod.

Walking away from the kitchen, I made my way to the washroom to drain my lizard, passing some people on the stairs, three to be exact, simply masturbating, two guys and girl, all watching each other. In the washroom, more specifically the tub, I saw a girl crouching over another girl's breasts and she was concentrating while the other girl gave her encouragement. "Come on Faith, you can do it, baby."

Flipping up the toilet seat, I held my girl in my hand and the two girls stopped to watch me. Not being bladder shy, I simply peed out what I'd apparently been holding since we left. It was a lot.

"Wow," said the one lying down. "Can you do that to me next time?"

Giving my cock a shake, "What?"

"Pee on me, I'd love it"

That was kind'a weird, "Really?"

The other girl, apparently figuring out that relaxing was the key, urinated all over her friend's breasts and she sighed contently as she kneaded it into her breasts and rubbed it all over her chest. I could only watch with muted interest. It was like a car crash and I couldn't look away. She finished up and then her lover went down and laid on top of her and they kissed, squishing the pee between each other's bodies, eventually rolling around in it. I decided to leave, and as I did I heard another hissing sound as the second girl went as well.

Casually looking at the rooms, whose doors had been taken off their hinges, I watched the various sexual deeds going on. Seeing as there where only three rooms there wasn't much sightseeing. The first room was actually empty, that was until I looked around the corner and saw two, no three guys fucking in a chain. I gave one of them a smile - the other two were busy with each other's assholes - which he returned, and my dick rose a little.

In the next room, a woman was chained down to the bed while a man was lashing at her pussy with a whip. She was crying out with each strike, but not out of pain, out of pleasure. If not for her screams of pleasure I would have cringed when he struck her breasts. But she seemed to revel in it, goading him on, "Yes! Yes! Harder!" My cock rose some more. The third and last room was…well it was romantic.

Two girls and a guy where making gentle love to each other, almost as if they'd practised before. One girl was sucking the other's breasts as the guy was slowly taking her from behind while they laid down on their sides. The one in the middle, slightly overweight and the other girl slim, seemed to be completely caught up in their movements. The intimacy and pleasure they were getting, although small but lasting, was beautiful. Not wanting to interrupt, I left them alone.

Grabbing my cock and pumping it as I walked was a new experience and by the time I reached the stairs, my erection was firm and ready, and nearly poked out the eye of a guy walking up.

"Sorry," I blushed a little at the almost accident.

"It's ok." He simply took my cock in his mouth and began giving me a blow job from the stairs.

Pulling her out of his mouth, I motioned him to follow me and we went into the room with the three men. Pulling him down onto the bed, ignoring the still fucking men, I reversed myself so we were both looking at the other's cock. Grabbing his now erect member, I licked the sensitive head and then pulled down the foreskin and kissed it up and down. He was not as gentle and he simply took me in his mouth, which was quite a feat as I'm not average, but he seemed not to notice as he put a finger at my back door as if waiting for an invitation. Pushing my ass at him he quickly pushed in and I felt my second anal penetration that night.

Dropping my mouth over his cock, I began pumping him and sucking him up and down as he pushed his finger deep inside my guy pussy and then added another finger, all the while licking and sucking my cock. He was an expert. My god he was an expert. I knew I wouldn't last long at this rate, but that didn't matter anymore. A hand touched my breast and then another touched my other one and suddenly I was aware of the other guys around us touching, kissing, or feeling me up.

I was in bliss. It was a cock party and mine was the centre of attention as they kissed it, licked it and stroked me over and over until finally I popped my head up off his cock and screamed out loud. "I'm cumming!" He grabbed my ass as I thrust deep into his throat and came harder and longer than I had in a while.

Pulling myself out of him, he was grinning as he shared some of the cum with the guys who kissed him. One of them pushed me up against the wall on the bed and kissed me, tasting his cock on my lips, as I tasted the one on his. He grabbed my breasts and kneaded them hard and long making me moan into him, his cock pressed against my chest. "Fuck me," I moaned, not caring what I said to him at the moment.

Wasting no time, he lifted up my soft girl cock and inserted himself into my guy pussy without fanfare and proceeded to fuck me up against the wall. My eyes half open, my mouth open with no words coming out as I was in a sexual haze just being fucked like a whore, and I loved every second of it. My body knew what to do even if my mind didn't and I was humping along with each thrust as he groaned out loud into me, firing off quickly. My cock was fully erect by that time and I was still not satisfied.

With a feral growl I said, "Bend over," and he did on all fours on the floor.

I had no mercy and took no quarter as I viciously rammed into his back door. He hissed in pain, saying, "Be gentle, please."

Completely taken over by Sexual Steph I said with a grin, "Are you an anal virgin? Is this the first cock you've had?"

He nodded and bit his lip in pain, making me groan out loud at the sight of it. Oh he was so cute when he did that. "Do you like my cock in your ass? Do you want to be fucked with my girlcock?" He nodded but didn't say anything as he was still biting his lip.

"What was that?" I asked, slowing down my pace, enjoying the power I had over him.

"Y-yes! Fuck me like a whore! Fuck my boy pussy!"

Grinning, I sped up and viciously assaulted his asshole as he and I groaned out loud as my full twelve inches penetrated a man's ass. Being not my girlfriend and not pregnant, I rammed into him like I was a woman possessed. He was tight like a vice, but my girl had cum three times already and I was lasting a little longer with each one. That was until someone said something from the door.

"Oh fuck him, Steph. Do him like he's your bitch."

Looking up, I realized it was Tiffany and she was naked, except for the thong and watching me with a grin on her face and a remote in her hand hooked up to a cord that went behind her. My lover watching me as I plowed a complete stranger was just so taboo and wrong and kinky! I fired off deep into his ass and we collapsed on the floor, nearly satisfied.

Tiffany came down to us and kissed him on the lips in front of me, watching me the whole time. It was so sexy I could only watch as my dick grew, coated in my recent cumming. She grabbed his dick and began masturbating him as he grabbed her breast and began kneading her flesh. She groaned and he groaned, and I groaned with them when a third mouth came down to clean me off, a male one.

"That is so hot," Tiffany said in the middle of a gasp. Bringing her head closer to me, pressing our breasts against the one guy's head in the middle, he didn't seem to mind, we kissed deeply.

Her lips tasted like a woman's cum and our tongues battled each other like they were sword fighters. Feeling her body against mine sharpened my nipples as we were like this for a few more moments, her chest rubbing against mine, nipples rubbing against each other's shooting electricity down my body each time they touched. My sensitive nipples were aching to be kissed, licked, sucked, something!

Someone squeezed my cock, making me break the kiss in shock as the guy who was licking me pointed to the one between us. He had passed out.

"He came," said Tiff as she let go of his dick, her hand covered in the aftermath. She was surprised she hadn't noticed it.

Smiling like a horny teenager, "Taste it," she said to me and we shared a little snack over top of the unconscious man.

The guy watched us for a bit with a limp cock and we put on a show for him, kissing and licking each other. I kissed her on the neck like she was my meal, making her crazy and moaning out loud. She quickly had an orgasm and I followed not a minute afterwards.

We both laid down side-by-side holding hands. All that could be heard was the faint buzzing coming from her backside. She grabbed the remote and switched it to a lower setting. We couldn't hear it anymore but we could feel the faint buzzing through the floor.

"You two were so hot," said someone.

Looking up, I found it was the guy who had given me the tongue bath. My blush returned as Sexual Steph had left the body for the moment, probably to recharge her batteries. "Oh thanks."

"You're blushing, now?"

Tiffany laughed out loud. "She's not normally so bold and brazen." She squeezed my hand for support. "But get her horny and she changes into a fierce sexual goddess."

"I noticed, you were an animal"

My face flushed red, "Thanks."

"My name's Todd. How do you know Lacy?"

"She's a co-worker," supplied Tiffany.

"Oh, she's my cousin."

Really? "Cousin?"

He laughed, "Yeah, but we don't do stuff. We've known each other too long, it would be weird."

Tiffany wiggled her hips a little, "Not that weird."

"Oh yeah it would. I changed her diapers" I laughed out loud, so did she then he did too.

That made the guy who passed out wake up, "Huh? What?"

"Morning, hon," said the guy.

"Hey sweetie," he said without moving, "My ass hurts."

We all shared another laugh at that.

THE END

Here is a sample from another story you may enjoy:

SCOUT ALLEN

One of a Kind

Lesbian Erotica

SHE WALKED to the frame she was working on, torch and materials in hand. She placed them both down near the frame before welding.

A pink hardhat came up onto the welder and placed a toolbox down near her, waiting until she was finished, careful to keep his eyes away from the welder's spark.

"Hey, we finished work an hour ago. Let's go!"

Grunting as she finished, she flipped up her mask, and a female face looked at the male's, partially hidden underneath his pink hardhat. "Just finishing up the last touches," she told him with a smile. "You know how I am." She picked up her tools and took off the welder's mask, then twisted off the tanks of propane and acetylene.

"Okay, let's book it."

The pair walked off the construction site and into the same car, heading to the bar that they loved to go to. One for the food, the other for the waitress.

A smiling woman, just a year away from being thirty, greets the pair as they take a table in her section. It was a quiet Monday and they had air around them to talk.

"Hey Candice, Heath. How's it going?"

~=*0*=~

Leanne had been wondering when the two would show up; it was an hour later than when they usually showed up and she had been waiting to see her friend Candice, who always seemed to brighten her day.

"It's going good," replied Heath.

"A late finish today," explained Candice, "had to weld up a frame. I didn't want to leave it unfinished until tomorrow."

After her friend's explanation, she breathed a sigh of relief. She understood the dangers of their work, and her mind had concocted many horrible reasons why they hadn't shown up.

"Oh, well I'm glad it wasn't anything serious."

Leanne took their orders then went and punched them in, before checking on her other tables.

Heath watched the waitress go, pondering the worry he had caught in her voice.

When Leanne came back to them to talk about her morning - something about a horrible woman who had come in for lunchtime - Heath watched them without saying a word.

These two women, he observed, were seemingly opposites in their personality and lifestyles. But somehow, they had formed a bond that he wasn't sure they themselves were completely aware of. Leanne, with her uncertainties and turbulent emotions about anything that distressed her, was able to talk to Candice. In turn, Candice, with her steadfast sense of self and blunt way of dealing with her emotions, offered her advice in a very direct way that seemed to help her.

He was no stranger to watching the two women relate with each other. Yet over the last two months he'd seen something a little bit more intimate than normal. It started with a touch on the shoulder here and a playful swat there, and then Leanne would put her hand on Candice's leg for a moment longer than necessary. This part was most odd because Candice hadn't expressed an interest in women, at least she hadn't told him about it, but she never pulled away or asked Candice to remove it, and they would continue to talk normally as if it were natural.

Taking a drink of water, he noticed Leanne's hand disappear underneath the table to touch her friend's leg again and Candice gave her a warmer smile. Then they continued talking as if nothing had happened.

He looked up at another waitress he knew well, one he was truly trying to move past the barrier of friendship with, and saw that she had seen as well. They exchanged looks of knowing.

If you enjoyed this sample then look for **Both Ways**.

Also by this Author

About the Author

I've been writing for about thirteen years now but have never published anything, until recently.

I'm open for some creative criticisms to help move my stories from young hopeful to mature writer.

I LOVE playing video games, yes criticize me if you want but I love them, and my favorite original game is Assassin's Creed for putting the assassin in a position of honor and heroics. Some of my greatest influences come from video games, pictures, movies, books, random things like how something looks at a particular part of the day, manga, and anime.

Anime is the Japanese animated cartoons; Manga is the paper version (I hate it when people get it mixed up) and I like the ridiculousness of them and the imagination put into them because it's nothing like any cartoons you find in Canada. There's a freedom of expression in it I find so freeing, I dare you to tell me of another culture as expressive.

I obviously love writing, and I also like reading but find it very hard to find books that are engaging. Unless a book captures my attention right off the bat, I tend not to read it and it gets put on the backburner of my "to read" list.

I love listening to music when I write stories and often play scenes of my stories in my mind, mainly the action ones. It really helps me visualize them and get a good feel for them.

I like most music, even rap and country ones that I think people judge too harshly. And I draw inspiration from them as well.

As always read, live, laugh, and enjoy life to the fullest whenever you can. Peace!

Check my page on Amazon and my blog for Updates and interesting info.

Author Central - http://www.amazon.com/Scout-Allen/e/B00A48L3EU
Author Blog - http://scout-allen.awesomeauthors.org/

If you enjoyed any of my books then please share the love and click like on my books in Amazon.

If you write me a review and send me an email I will send you a free book, or many.
(Just know that these emails are filtered by my publisher.)

Good news is always welcome.

One Last Thing, For Kindle Readers...

When you turn the page, Kindle will give you the opportunity to rate this book and share your thoughts on Facebook and Twitter. If you enjoyed my writings, would you please take a few seconds to let your friends know about it? Because... when they enjoy they will be grateful to you and so will I.

Thank You!

Scout Allen
scout_allen@awesomeauthors.org